AW YEAH!

A HASBRO ACTION FIGURE JAM

Become our fan on Facebook **facebook.com/idwpublishing**
Follow us on Twitter **@idwpublishing**
Subscribe to us on YouTube **youtube.com/idwpublishing**
See what's new on Tumblr **tumblr.idwpublishing.com**
Check us out on Instagram **instagram.com/idwpublishing**

IDW
www.IDWPUBLISHING.com

Licensed By:

ISBN: 978-1-63140-987-5 20 19 18 17 1 2 3 4

AW YEAH!: HASBRO ACTION FIGURE JAM. OCTOBER 2017. FIRST PRINTING.

Originally published as REVOLUTION: AW YEAH! issues #1–3.

Special thanks to Hasbro's Derryl Depriest, David Erwin, Grant Gie, Ed Lane, Ben Montano, Beth Artale, Josh Feldman and Michael Kelly.

AW YEAH!

WRITTEN AND DRAWN BY
ART BALTAZAR

SERIES EDITS BY
DAVID HEDGECOCK

COLLECTION EDITS BY
JUSTIN EISINGER AND ALONZO SIMON

COLLECTION DESIGN BY
CLAUDIA CHONG

PUBLISHER:
TED ADAMS

ART BY ART BALTAZAR

IDW PROUDLY PRESENTS...

THE AW YEAH REVOLUTION! HAS BEGUN!
BY ART BALTAZAR
I TELL YOU, ANDROMEDA!
THIS SNAKE EYES CHARACTER IS PRETTY COOL!
WHAT A GUY!
I NEED HIM IN MY COLLECTION!
AW YEAH REVOLUTION!

SNAKE EYES IS MY FAVORITE SUPER HERO FOR SURE!
AW YEAH REVOLUTION!
BUT, HENCE!
CHILLAXING TIME HAS COME TO AN END, GOOD BROTHER!
OUR EVIL BIDDING AND PLANNING MUST CONTINUE!
I PROPOSE OUR FIRST MISSION IS TO ACQUIRE THE ULTIMATE POWER IN THE UNIVERSE!
BUT WHERE DO WE START, YOU ASK?
I HAVE LOCATED THIS POWER IN A NEARBY SYSTEM!
A SOLAR SYSTEM TO BE PRECISE!

MORE PRECISELY...
...EARTH!
THAT'S WHAT THEY CALL IT!
AND HIDDEN WITHIN THIS EARTH...
...IS THE ORBSAH GEM! THE MYSTICAL ANCIENT ARTIFACT!
IT JUST SO HAPPENS TO BE THE TOPIC OF CONTROVERSY AMONG SOME GIANT ROBOT BEINGS!
THOSE DREADED TRANSFORMERS!
HA!
THEY WILL BE NO MATCH FOR THE MIGHT OF THE EVIL BARON KARZA!
AND YOU, TOO, ANDROMEDA.
PET PET
HA!
AND TOGETHER, WE CAN CAUSE MUCH CHAOS!

MEANWHILE IN ANOTHER PART OF THE GALAXY...
...WE JOIN ROM ON HIS NEVERENDING SEARCH ACROSS THE UNIVERSE FOR THE EVIL AND NASTY...
DIRE WRAITHS!
I THINK I'M CLOSING IN ON THOSE EVIL CREATURES!
THERE!
THAT LONE ASTEROID!
I'M SENSING SOMETHING CREEPY HAPPENING OVER THERE!
PING
PING
PING PING
PING
THIS DESERVES A CLOSER LOOK!
THE READING IS VERY STRONG!
PING
PING
PING

WOOT!
AH!
THERE ARE THE CREEPS I KNOW!
HEY!
CALM DOWN, FELLAS!
LET'S TALK ABOUT THIS!
YOU MUST STOP THREATENING THE HUMAN RACE!

WE CAN DO THIS THE EASY WAY, Y'KNOW.
BLAHR!
BLARG!
BLARGH! BLARGH!
OKAY, HERE WE GO!
THWAP!
BLARGH!
THWAP!

THE HARD WAY IT IS!
FIGHT!
FIGHT!
IT'S TIME FOR MY OWN PERSONAL FORCE FIELD!
VVZZZHMMMMMM!

WHAT THE--?!
MY SENSORS ARE DETECTING A MINIATURE BEING!
WHO ARE YOU?
I AM BARON KARZA, FOOL!
AND YOU WILL COME WITH ME!
AARGH!
?
?
?
?
?

ELSEWHERE...
BOOM!!
WATCH OUT!
COBRA'S ATTACKING!

CURSE YOU, G.I. JOES!
EXPLODE!
PEW!
PEW!
PEW!
PEW!
PEW!
EXPLODE!
EXPLODE!
PEW!
PEW!
PEW!
IT'S AN AMBUSH!
TIME TO CALL FOR BACKUP!
PEW!
EXPLODE!

MR. SNAKE EYES...
...IT'S AN HONOR TO BE IN YOUR PRESENCE.
PLEASE FORGIVE ME.
BUT YOU MUST COME WITH ME!
ZZZMM!
SNAKE EYES?

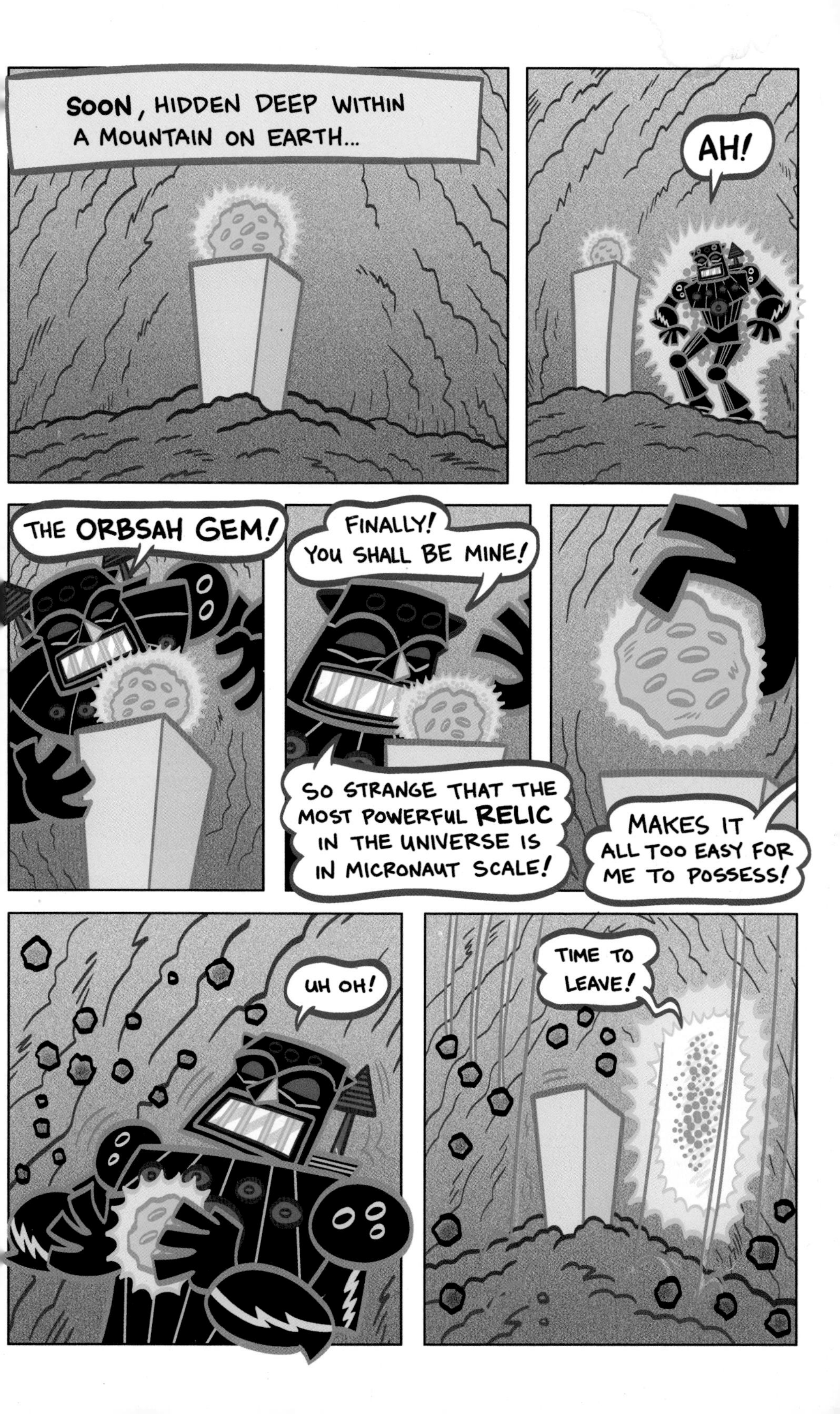
SOON, HIDDEN DEEP WITHIN A MOUNTAIN ON EARTH...
AH!
THE ORBSAH GEM!
FINALLY! YOU SHALL BE MINE!
SO STRANGE THAT THE MOST POWERFUL RELIC IN THE UNIVERSE IS IN MICRONAUT SCALE!
MAKES IT ALL TOO EASY FOR ME TO POSSESS!
UH OH!
TIME TO LEAVE!

WHILE OUTSIDE...
WHAT?
AN EARTHQUAKE!
THE MOUNTAIN IS CRUMBLING!
TRANSFORMERS, ROLL OUT!
ONE MORE THING BEFORE I GO!
YOU MUST COME WITH ME!

AARGHH!
OPTIMUS?

ELSEWHERE...
UHG!
WHERE AM I?
I'M ENCASED IN SOME KIND OF FORCE BUBBLE!
HA!
THAT'S CORRECT, FOOL!
SAY HELLO TO YOUR CAPTURED NEIGHBORS!
SNAKE EYES...
...AND OPTIMUS PRIME!
THIS IS THE ORBSAH GEM!
AND WITH THIS...
I SHALL DRAIN YOUR POWERS!

YOUR SPACE TRACKING SKILLS!
YOUR AMAZING ALT-MODE!
AND YOUR COOLNESS!
AND TOGETHER... WITH YOUR POWERS...
I WILL CONTROL THE UNIVERSE!
HA HA HEE HOH!

ELSEWHERE, IN MICROSPACE...
ACROYEAR!
SOMETHING IS DISRUPTING THE BALANCE OF MICROSPACE!
LOOKS LIKE SUPER-SIZED BEINGS!
I SEE.
YES.
OUR HORIZON HAS BEEN ALTERED!
ANY MORE SUPER-SIZED BEINGS CAN DESTROY THE MOLECULAR DENSITY OF OUR UNIVERSE!
THERE'S ONLY ONE VILLAIN WHO WOULD TRY SOMETHING LIKE THIS!
BARON KARZA!

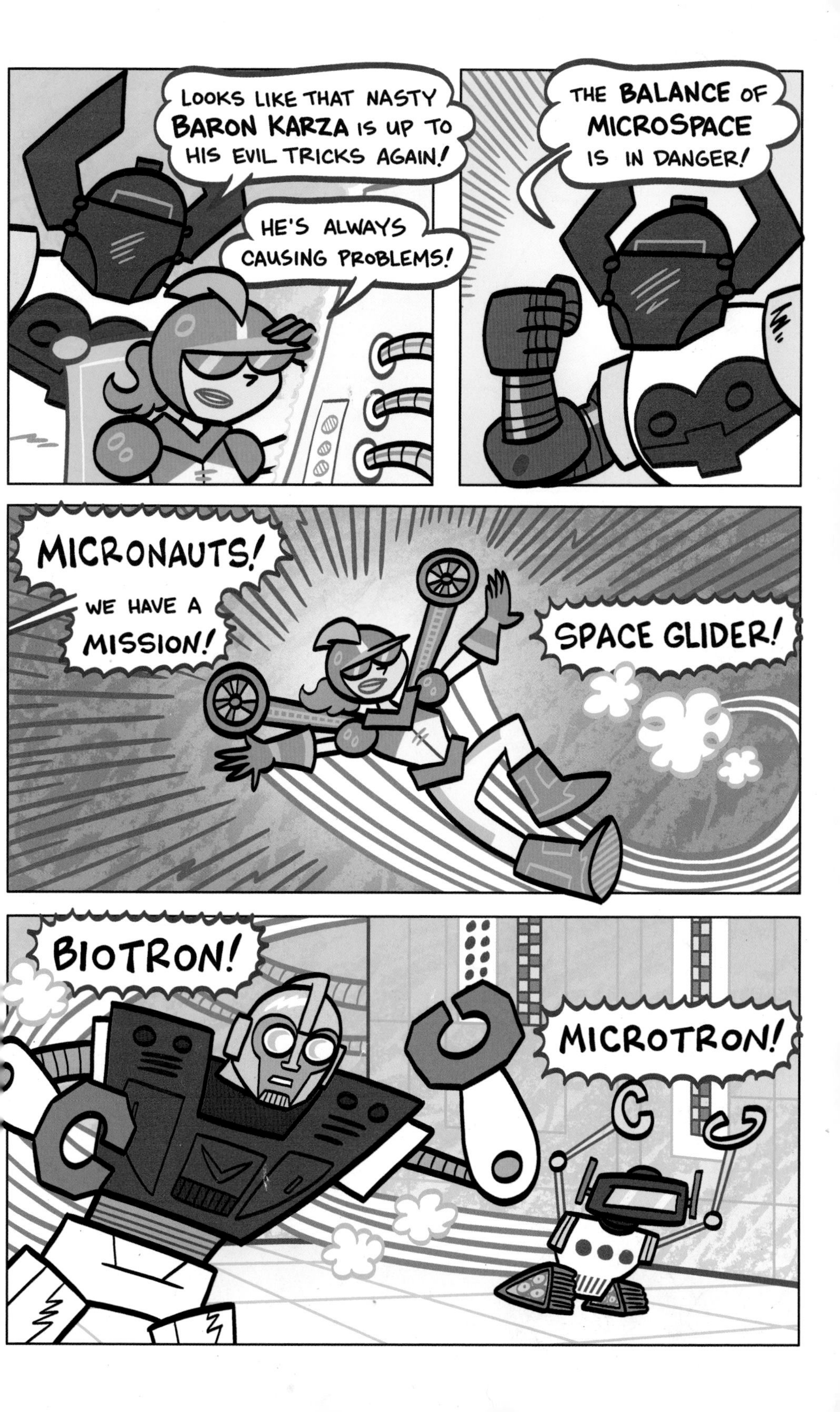
LOOKS LIKE THAT NASTY BARON KARZA IS UP TO HIS EVIL TRICKS AGAIN!
HE'S ALWAYS CAUSING PROBLEMS!
THE BALANCE OF MICROSPACE IS IN DANGER!
MICRONAUTS!
WE HAVE A MISSION!
SPACE GLIDER!
BIOTRON!
MICROTRON!

OUR CALL TO ACTION IS NOW!
AW YEAH TO BE CONTINUED!

ART BY **ART BALTAZAR**

MEANWHILE, IN MICROSPACE...
OUR HEROES...
OPTIMUS PRIME...
...ROM...
...AND SNAKE EYES...
...HAVE JUST FALLEN VICTIMS TO THE POWER OF THE ORBSAH GEM!
VVZZHHZ!!

AW YEAH
REVOLUTION!
BY ART BALTAZAR
EDITED BY
DAVID HEDGECOCK

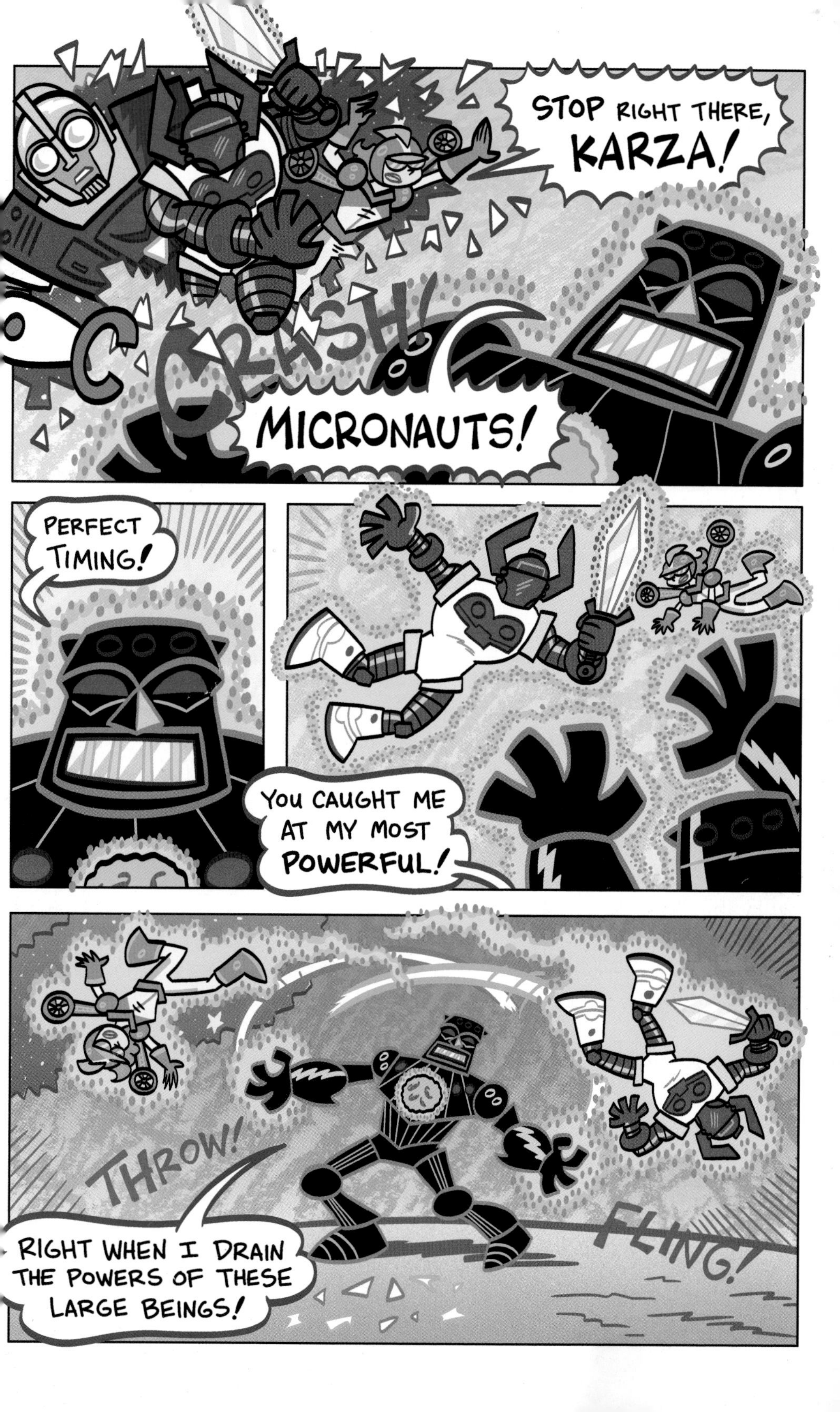
STOP RIGHT THERE, KARZA!
CRASH!
MICRONAUTS!
PERFECT TIMING!
YOU CAUGHT ME AT MY MOST POWERFUL!
THROW!
FLING!
RIGHT WHEN I DRAIN THE POWERS OF THESE LARGE BEINGS!

BIOTRON!
BRING IT, BIG GUY!
STOP THIS FOOLISHNESS, KARZA!
STOMP!
LEAP!
I CALL UPON THE POWER OF OPTIMUS PRIME!
GROW!
GROW!
WHAT THE--?
YOU CAN GROW NOW?
THAT'S NEW!
YOU WILL FIND THE ORBSAH GEM'S ABILITIES QUITE AMAZING!

TTRRNSFFRRMMMMM!!
UGHNN!
LOOK! MICROTRON ENTERS THE SCENE!
HA! BIOTRON!
YOU ARE FINISHED!

THE LITTLE ROBOT RUSHES TO FREE THE GIANT BEINGS FROM THEIR SPHERICAL PRISON!
CLICK
CLICK!
WONDROUS!
SOMETHING'S HAPPENING TO THE ENERGY BUBBLES!
POP!
POP!
POP!
WE'RE FREE!

NOW, LET'S DISCOVER MORE OF THIS MICRO WORLD!
STOMP!
QUAKE!
I DETECT INSTABILITY IN THIS WORLD'S DENSITY!
QUAKE!
RUMBLE!
RUMBLE!
SHAKE!
QUAKE!
YEAH.
THAT SEEMS TO BE A BIG PROBLEM.
RUMBLE!
SHAKE!
SEE, KARZA?!
IT'S YOUR FAULT!
YOUR EVIL WAYS ARE DESTROYING OUR WORLD!

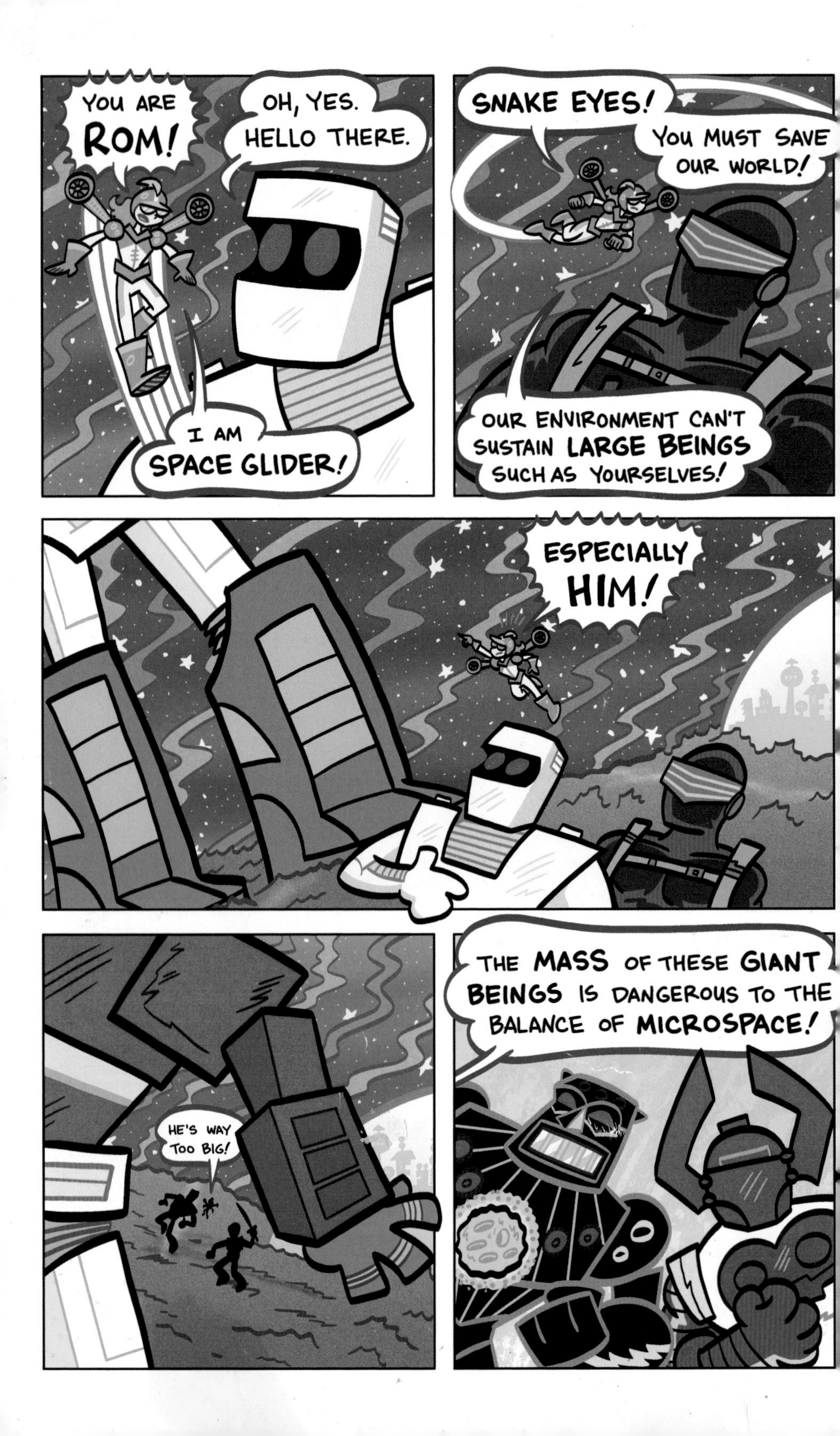
YOU ARE ROM!
OH, YES. HELLO THERE.
I AM SPACE GLIDER!
SNAKE EYES!
YOU MUST SAVE OUR WORLD!
OUR ENVIRONMENT CAN'T SUSTAIN LARGE BEINGS SUCH AS YOURSELVES!
ESPECIALLY HIM!
HE'S WAY TOO BIG!
THE MASS OF THESE GIANT BEINGS IS DANGEROUS TO THE BALANCE OF MICROSPACE!

WELL, IF THAT'S THE SITUATION...
SHOVE!
HEY!
VVZHT!
...I NO LONGER HAVE USE FOR THIS REALM!
IT'S TIME FOR THE VILLAIN TO MAKE HIS EXIT!
CURSE YOU, HEROES!

MEANWHILE, SOMEWHERE ON EARTH...
...IN A SECRET LOCATION...
... IS A SECRET COBRA FORTRESS...
THE COBRA NINJA KNOWN AS STORM SHADOW MEDITATES ATOP HIS FAVORITE MOUNTAIN...
WHEN SUDDENLY...
VVZZHHMMM!!

VVZZZ
WHAT'S THIS?!!
COBRA IS UNDER ATTACK!!
SO BE IT!

WHILE IN MICROSPACE...
QUICKLY!
THROUGH THE PORTAL! YOU LARGE BEINGS MUST RETURN TO YOUR OWN WORLD!
MY SWORD'S ENERGY IS KEEPING THE PORTAL FROM CLOSING!
GO! GO! GO!
HURRY!
WE'RE THROUGH!
WE MEET AGAIN, SNAKE EYES!
MY MORTAL ENEMY!
I SHOULD HAVE KNOWN IT WAS YOU BEHIND THIS MONSTROSITY!

YOUR FELLOW JOES WERE FOOLS TO SEND THAT WEAPON HERE!
THEY THINK THEY CAN DEFEAT COBRA?
WEAPON? WHAT WEAPON?
THE GIGANTIC ROBOT KNOWN AS OPTIMUS PRIME!
WE TOOK HIM DOWN SWIFTLY!
IT WAS CHALLENGING, BUT COBRA WAS SUCCESSFUL!
WITH SOME HELP FROM...
...THE EVIL KARZA!

GROW!
GROW!
NYAH HA HA!
GROW!
WHAT THE--?!
KARZA?
BUT KARZA WENT THROUGH THE PORTAL SECONDS BEFORE WE DID!
TIME IN MICROSPACE MOVES MUCH DIFFERENTLY THAN TIME ON EARTH!
YOU KNOW OF MICROSPACE?
YES INDEED. KARZA EXPLAINED IT WELL.

MUCH LIKE OUR WORLD'S DENSITY, TIME PASSES ACCORDING TO OUR SIZE AS WELL.
NOW, EXCUSE ME WHILE SNAKE EYES AND I CONTINUE WHERE WE LEFT OFF...
...THE BROTHERHOOD CHALLENGE OF DESTINY!
CLINK!
LOSER WILL MEET HIS DEMISE!
KICK!

HA HA HEE HOH!
BOUNCE!
FALL!
RECOVERY IS NOT IN YOUR FUTURE!
CLANG!
STOP THIS FOOLISHNESS, YOU EVIL THREAT!
WHAT SMALL IRRITANT IS THIS?
THIS IS A SITUATION FOR THE NEUTRALIZER!
A SPACEKNIGHT'S GREATEST WEAPON!
AWAY WITH YOU, VILLAIN!
ARGH!
BLAST!
BLAST!
BLAST!

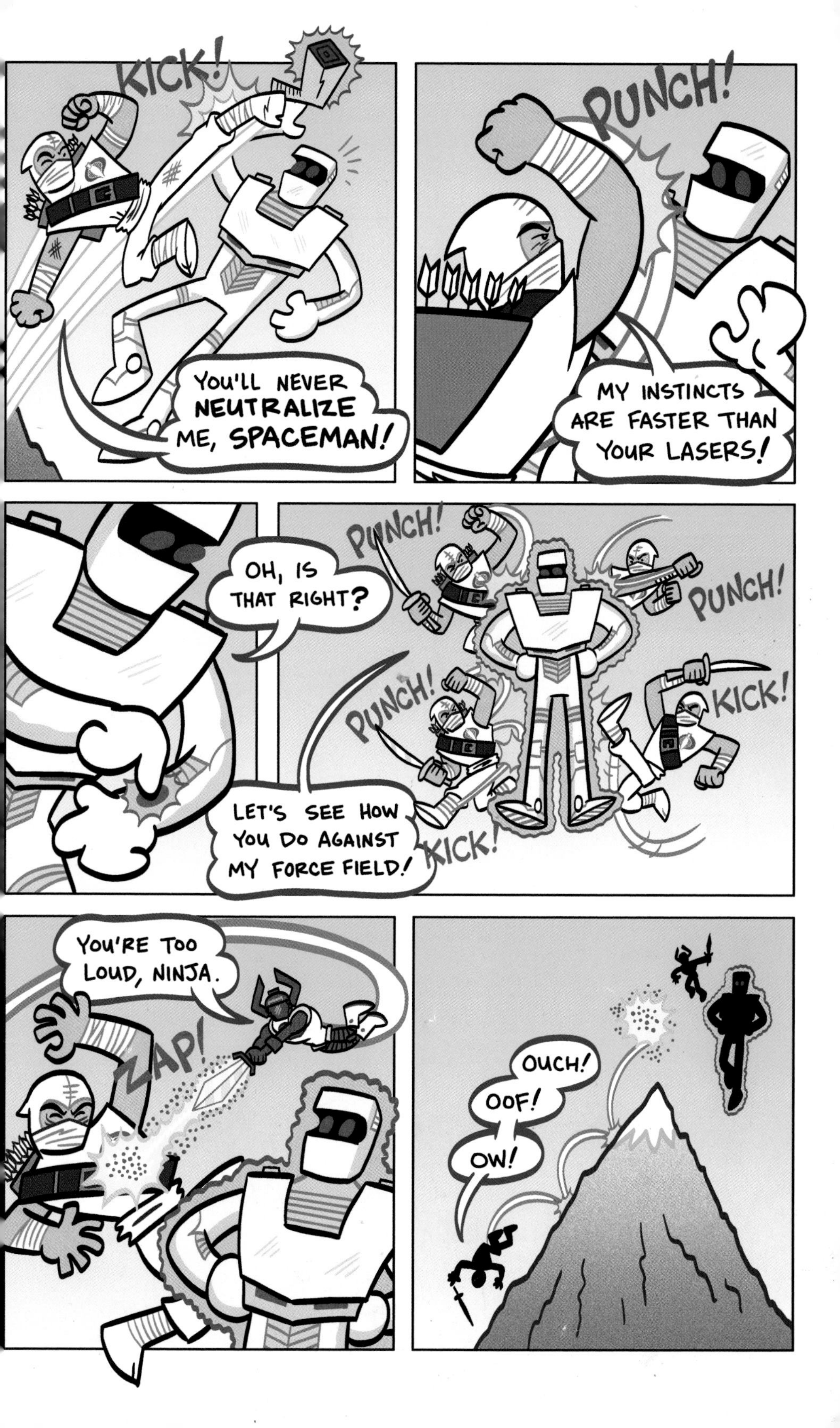
KICK!
YOU'LL NEVER NEUTRALIZE ME, SPACEMAN!
PUNCH!
MY INSTINCTS ARE FASTER THAN YOUR LASERS!
OH, IS THAT RIGHT?
PUNCH!
PUNCH!
PUNCH!
KICK!
KICK!
LET'S SEE HOW YOU DO AGAINST MY FORCE FIELD!
YOU'RE TOO LOUD, NINJA.
ZAP!
OUCH!
OOF!
OW!

UGH!
THAT SPACEMAN IS UNPREDICTABLE...
...BUT THAT MINI WARRIOR HAS INCREDIBLE POWER!
OH, RIGHT. I FORGOT ABOUT SNAKE EYES!
LET'S FINISH THIS WITH NO INTERRUPTIONS!
BBRMMMMMMMRRRRMMMMM

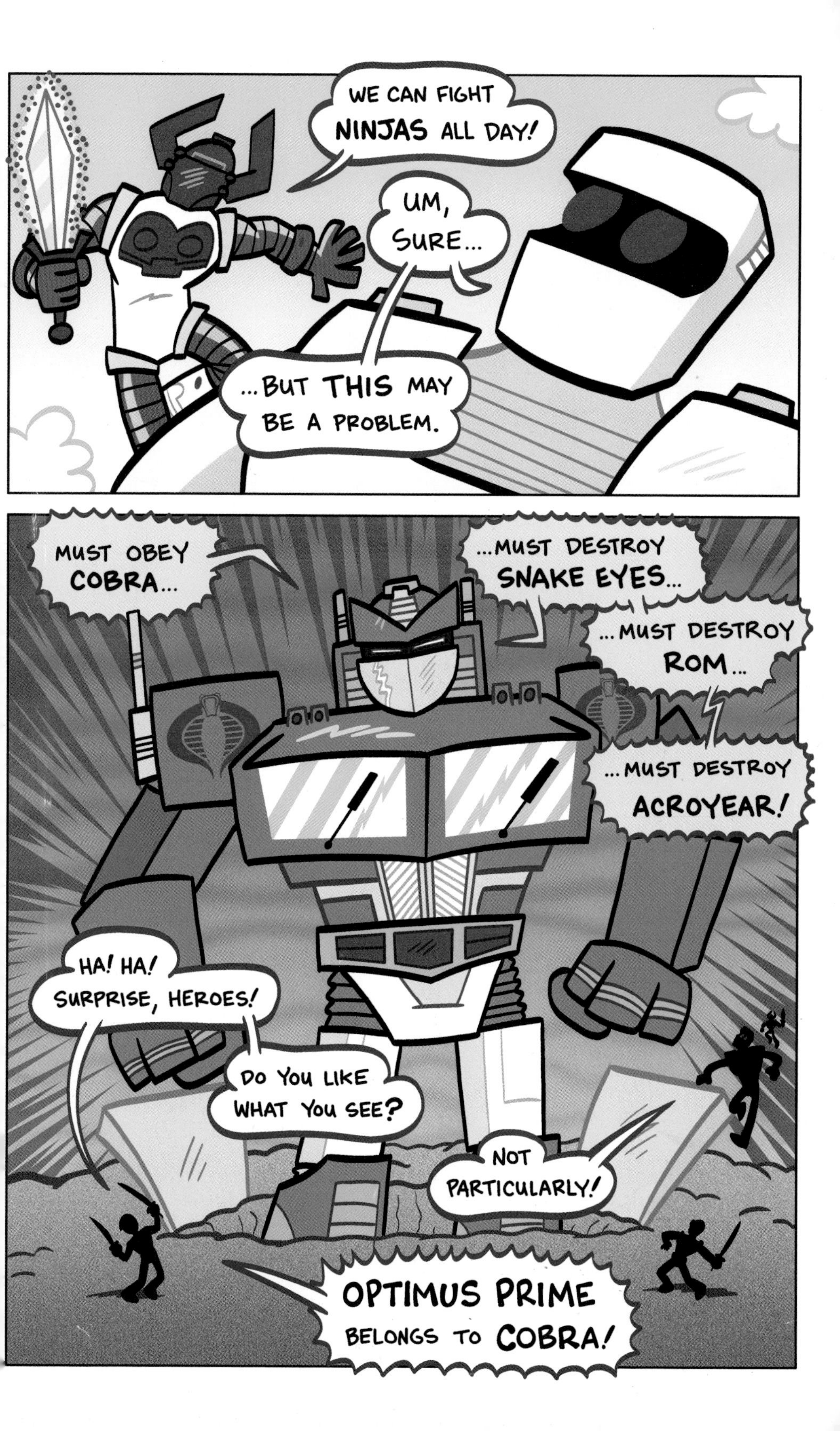
WE CAN FIGHT NINJAS ALL DAY!
UM, SURE...
...BUT THIS MAY BE A PROBLEM.
MUST OBEY COBRA...
...MUST DESTROY SNAKE EYES...
...MUST DESTROY ROM...
...MUST DESTROY ACROYEAR!
HA! HA! SURPRISE, HEROES!
DO YOU LIKE WHAT YOU SEE?
NOT PARTICULARLY!
OPTIMUS PRIME BELONGS TO COBRA!

MEANWHILE, IN THE FAR REACHES OF SPACE...
AN ASTEROID IS ON A COLLISION COURSE WITH EARTH...
BUT MORE IMPORTANT...
THE ASTEROID'S PASSENGERS.
THE EVIL ALIEN DIRE WRAITHS!
WE HAVE TRACKED OUR ENEMY...
ROM...
...TO THIS TINY BLUE PLANET!
WE ARE COMING FOR YOU, ROM!
YOUR DESTRUCTION IS NEAR!
HA HA HEE HOH!

ART BY **ART BALTAZAR**

IDW PROUDLY PRESENTS...
ZZZAPP!
BBZZZ
CLANG!
COBRA ATTACK!

AW YEAH
REVOLUTION!
BY ART BALTAZAR
EDITED BY
DAVID HEDGECOCK

OKAY, GUYS!
THIS LITTLE MISUNDERSTANDING IS GETTING RIDICULOUS!
GRRR!
VERY WELL...
FORCE FIELD UP!
HA! I CAN DO THIS FOREVER!
UNLESS I...
...REVERSE THE FORCE FIELD!
THAT SHOULD HOLD YOU GUYS!
NOW TAKE THIS TIME TO RELAX AND REFLECT UPON YOUR ACTIONS!

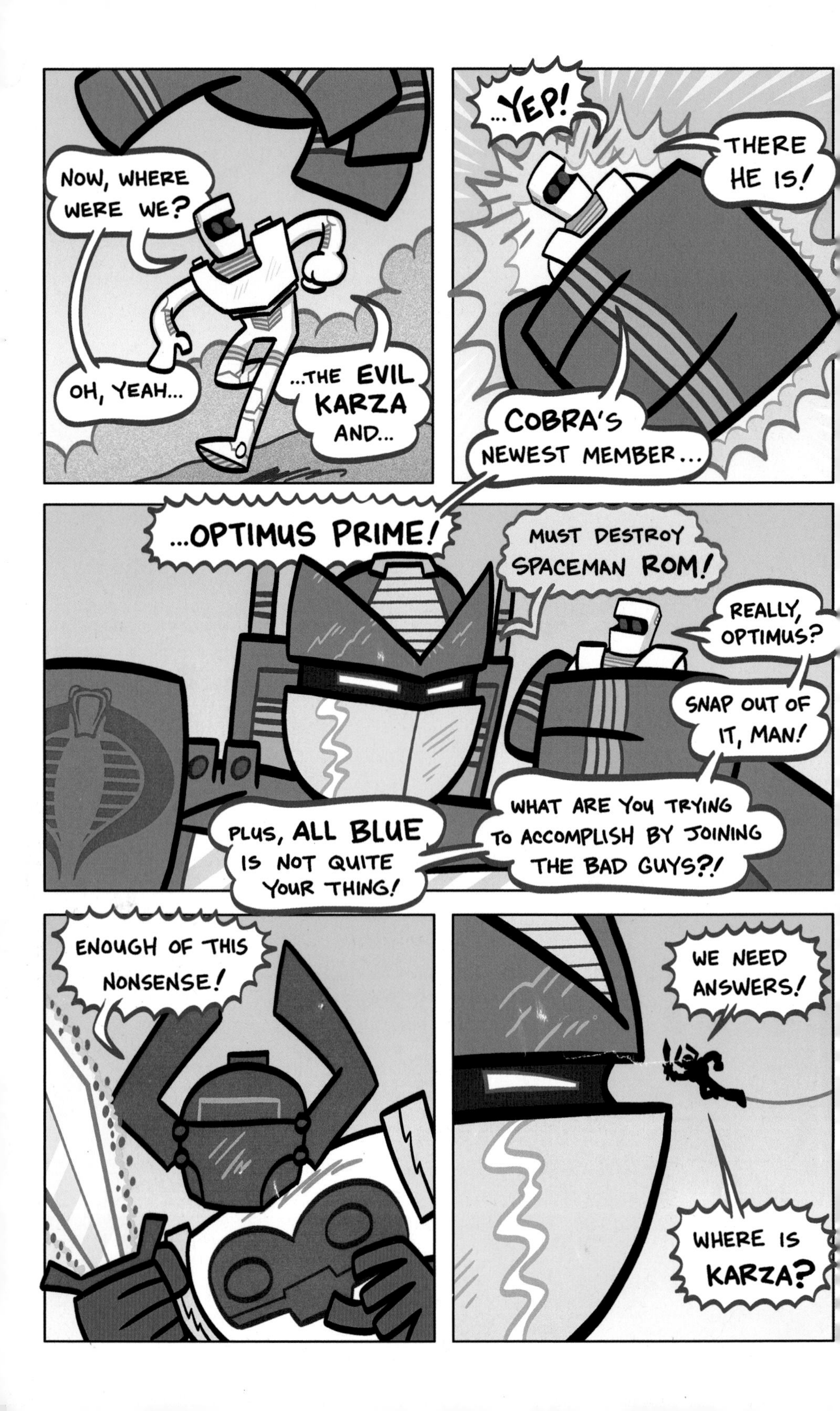
NOW, WHERE WERE WE?
OH, YEAH...
...THE EVIL KARZA AND...
...YEP!
THERE HE IS!
COBRA'S NEWEST MEMBER...
...OPTIMUS PRIME!
MUST DESTROY SPACEMAN ROM!
REALLY, OPTIMUS?
SNAP OUT OF IT, MAN!
WHAT ARE YOU TRYING TO ACCOMPLISH BY JOINING THE BAD GUYS?!
PLUS, ALL BLUE IS NOT QUITE YOUR THING!
ENOUGH OF THIS NONSENSE!
WE NEED ANSWERS!
WHERE IS KARZA?

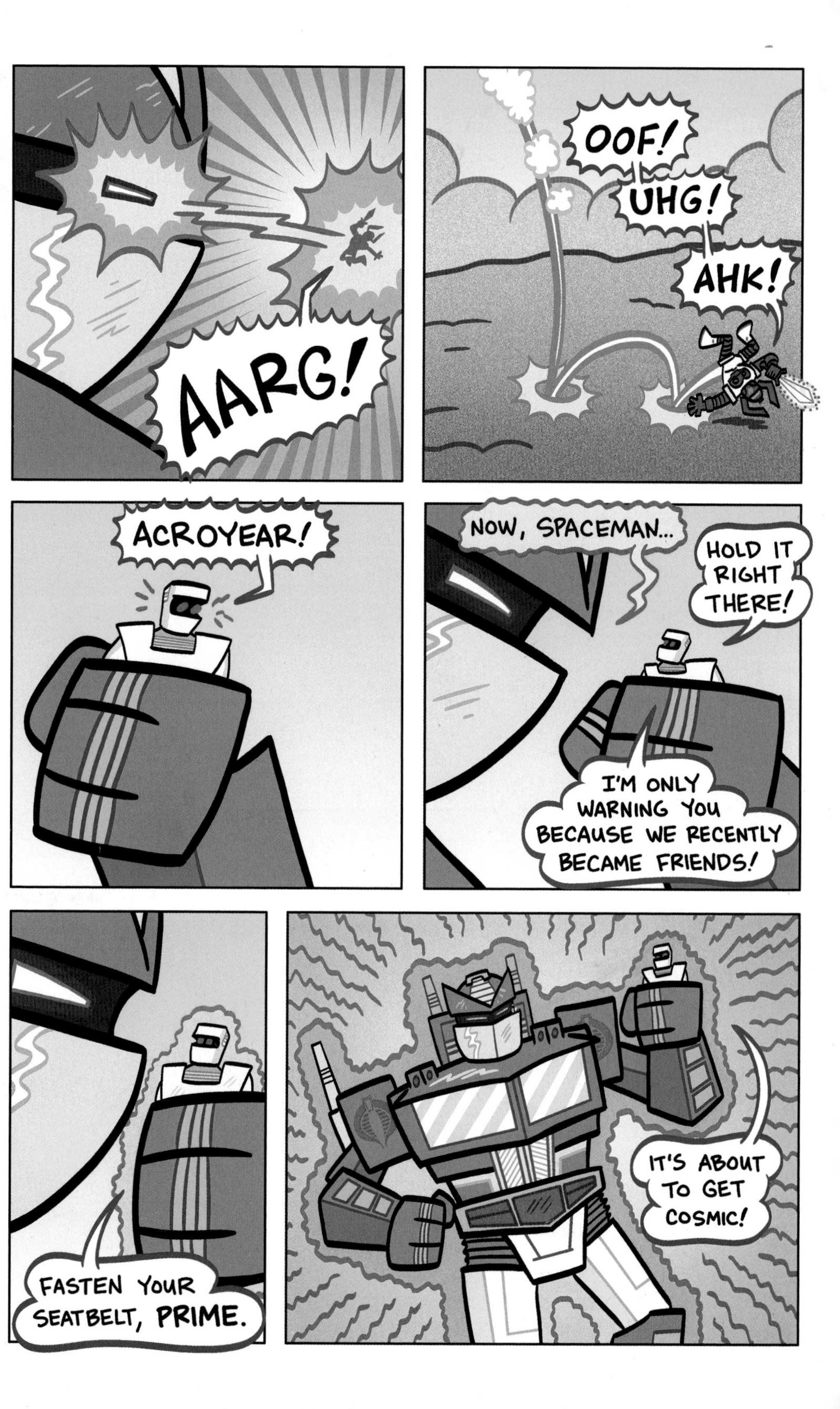
AARG!
OOF!
UHG!
AHK!
ACROYEAR!
NOW, SPACEMAN...
HOLD IT RIGHT THERE!
I'M ONLY WARNING YOU BECAUSE WE RECENTLY BECAME FRIENDS!
FASTEN YOUR SEATBELT, PRIME.
IT'S ABOUT TO GET COSMIC!

WHAT ARE YOU DOING?
WE ARE GOING FOR A RIDE!
OUT OF EARTH'S ATMOSPHERE!
BREAK!

LATER, OPTIMUS!
THIS SHOULD GET YOU WELL OUT OF RANGE OF COBRA'S CONTROL!
UH OH!
WHAT'S THIS?!
ANOTHER THREAT?

AN ASTEROID FILLED WITH THE EVIL ALIEN DIRE WRAITHS!
NYAH!
NYAH!
GRRNAH!
NOT GOOD!
AND IT'S HURTLING RIGHT TOWARDS EARTH!
CURSE YOU, ROM!
YOU WILL NOT STOP US!
YOU WILL FAIL!
ARG!
PREPARE TO MEET YOUR DEMISE!
MEANWHILE, ON EARTH...
... MEMBERS OF G.I. JOE RUSH INTO BATTLE TO HELP THEIR FRIEND SNAKE EYES...
... LED BY THE MICRONAUTS' SPACE GLIDER!

FOLLOW ME, SCARLETT!
WE GOT THIS!
WHAT'S GOING ON HERE?
STATUS REPORT!
WHILE COBRA ATTACKS, DESTRO JOINS THE FIGHT...
WHERE IS WEAPON PRIME?
THE SPACEMAN LAUNCHED HIM INTO ORBIT.
PRIME WILL RETURN. YOU'LL SEE!
WHAT DID I MISS, FELLAS?
KARZA!
YOU SEEM TALLER.
I AM!
IT'S THE POWER OF THE ORBSAH GEM!
NOW, OBSERVE!

HA!
I SHALL MENACE THEE!
AND THE WORLD WILL BE MINE!
HA HA HEE HOH!
AGAIN WITH THE WORLD DOMINATION?
WHAT IS IT WITH THESE BAD GUYS?
HE'S GIGANTIC!
SINCE WHEN CAN KARZA DO THAT?

NOW, MICRONAUTS!
YOU WILL FEEL THE WRATH OF...
AK!
KNOCK!
...THE DIRE WRAITHS?!
THUD!
TIME TO GET THIS GEM FAR AWAY FROM YOU, KARZA!
NO MORE POWER FOR YOU, EVIL ONE!
POP!

IT ENDS NOW, KARZA!
YOU'VE LAUGHED YOUR LAST EVIL LAUGH!
WHAT?!
I'M BACK TO NORMAL!
HA! FOOLISH ACROYEAR!
ALWAYS THE HERO!
BUT YOU SEE...
I DON'T NEED THE ORBSAH GEM TO DESTROY YOU!
YAH!
MY SWORD FIGHTING SKILLS SHALL PREVAIL!
MY POWERS ARE JUST AS MIGHTY AS YOURS!
I WILL RULE EARTH AND MICROSPACE!

UM... AREN'T WE FORGETTING SOMETHING?
Y'KNOW, THAT ASTEROID...
...THAT KNOCKED KARZA ON HIS HEAD...
...IS FILLED WITH EVIL DIRE WRAITHS!
AND THEY ARE LOOKING RATHER VICIOUS TODAY!
NOT TO WORRY...
...I HAVE THE NEUTRALIZER!
NOT THIS TIME, ROM!
ARG!
YOUR SOUL BELONGS TO US!

THESE SOLDIER MINIONS WILL BUILD OUR ARMY VERY WELL!
ARG!
RETREAT!
RETREAT!
RULING THE UNIVERSE ONE BEING AT A TIME...
...IS GETTING EASIER AND EASIER!
AK!
NO!
AHK!
HMM...
...THE BATTLE TO RULE ALL EXISTENCE HAS GROWN TO UNIVERSAL PROPORTIONS!
THESE ALIENS ARE IMPRESSIVE.
MONSTERS!
AH!
HELP!
AHK!
I, DESTRO...
...NEED AN ADVANTAGE.

WHAT'S THIS?
WHAT HAS FATE BROUGHT ME TODAY?
AH.
THE ANCIENT ORBSAH GEM.
THE SOURCE OF IMMENSE POWER.
WHAT CAN IT DO?
ANYTHING I WANT.
IF FATE WILL HAVE ME AS RULER...
DESTRO?
...THEN MY ANSWER IS...
...YES!

OH NO!
THIS IS NOT GOOD!
TIME'S UP WRAITHS!
LET'S GO FOR A SPIN!
CURSE YOU, ROM!
THAT GEM IS CAUSING ALL KINDS OF PROBLEMS!
AND BESIDES, IT DOESN'T BELONG TO YOU!
HA!
IT CHOSE ME!
FINDERS KEEPERS, SPACEMAN!

THE ORBSAH GEM IS THE REASON OUR WORLDS ARE CLASHING!
THESE WRAITHS WANT TO DESTROY ME AND TAKE OVER EARTH!
SOUNDS LIKE JEALOUSY TO ME!
STAY OUT OF MY BUSINESS!
GO BACK TO WHERE YOU BELONG!
THE COSMOS MISSES YOU!
WAIT!
BLINK!
THE WRAITHS!
HEY!
THAT'S MY GEM!
THAT POWER BELONGS TO ME, DESTRO!
GO AWAY, KARZA!
WE DON'T NEED YOU ANYMORE!

GO BACK FROM WHENCE YOU CAME!
BLINK
WHAT THE--?
WE'RE BACK IN MICROSPACE!
IT'S ALL YOUR FAULT, KARZA!
SEE, YA!
BACK ON EARTH...
DESTRO AND COBRA WILL REIGN SUPREME!
NOTHING CAN STOP US NOW!
WE WILL MAKE THESE ALIEN WRAITHS OUR SERVANTS!
NOT EVEN G.I. JOE!

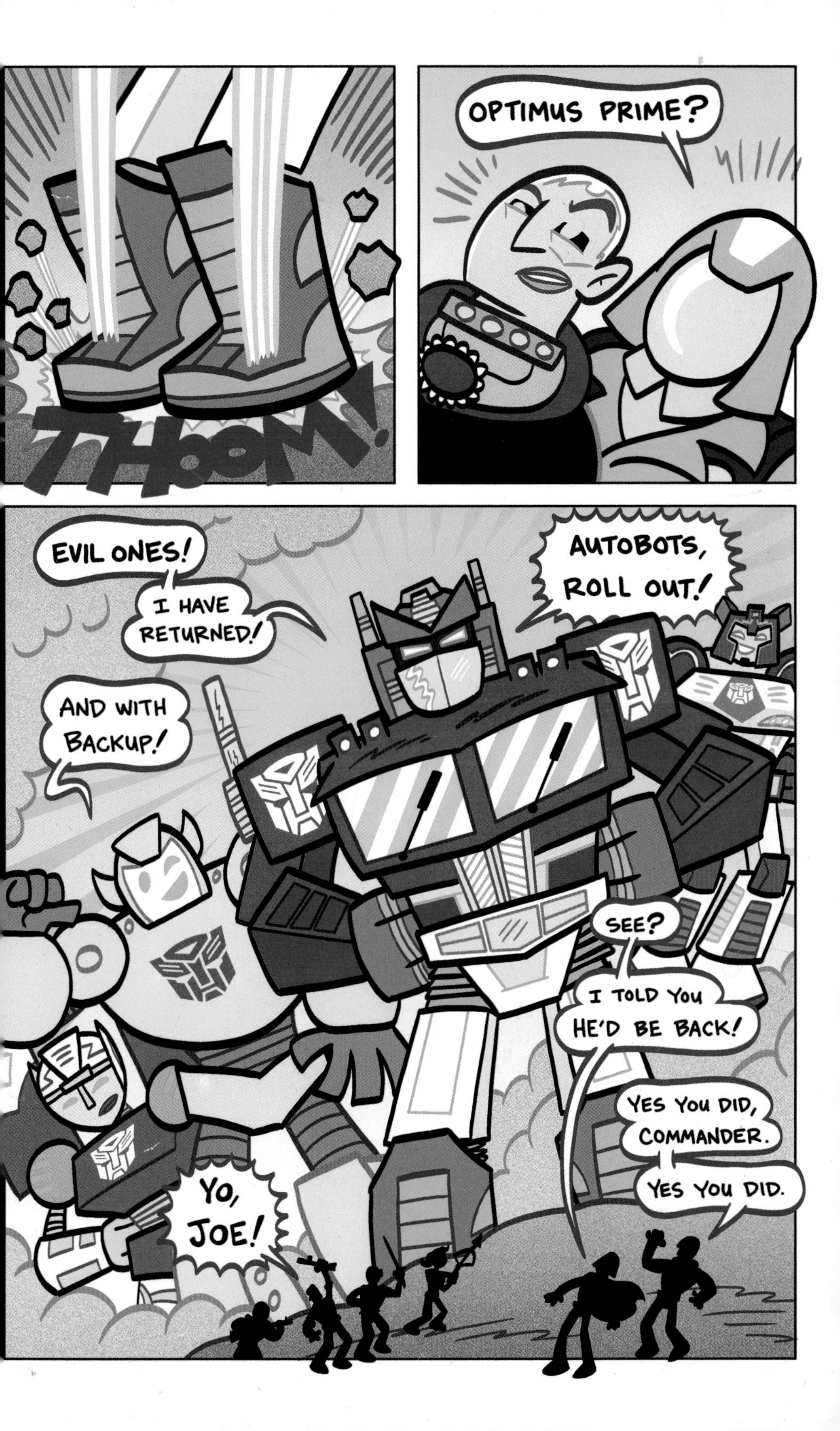
THOOM!
OPTIMUS PRIME?
EVIL ONES!
I HAVE RETURNED!
AUTOBOTS, ROLL OUT!
AND WITH BACKUP!
SEE?
I TOLD YOU HE'D BE BACK!
YES YOU DID, COMMANDER.
YES YOU DID.
YO, JOE!

SOMEWHERE IN THE FAR REACHES OF SPACE...
BLINK!
WHERE AM I?
MY SENSORS TELL ME I'M GALAXIES AWAY!
SENSORS ALSO INDICATE...
...THE DIRE WRAITHS ARE STILL ON EARTH!
AS LONG AS THOSE EVIL ALIENS EXIST...
...THE UNIVERSE IS DOOMED!
THE END?

ART BY JAY FOSGITT

ART BY FRANCO

ART BY FRANCO

ART BY FRANCO